# His & Hers

## Adventure

Made in Charleston, SC
www.PalmettoPublishingGroup.com

*His & Hers Adventure*
© 2020 by Benjamin Pell



Paperback: 978-1-64111-792-0
Hardback: 978-1-64111-799-9
eBook: 978-1-64111-793-7

# His & Hers Adventure

## Benjamin Pell

Once,

in a time not now,

in a place not here...

There lived a girl.
A girl unlike any other
for she had been born with
green skin and a pair of
horns atop her head.

Unique by any standard.

She grew up in a
small town just a
stones throw from
the middle
of nowhere.

No parents.

No friends.

The people called her
wildchild or beastling.

But she didn't care.
She spent her days dreaming
of lands far away.

Of a life filled with excitement and wonder.

The girl had woken up cold,
like she always did.
She had bathed in the river,
like she always did.
And was about to go to the square
to scavenge for scraps,
like she always did,
when it happened.

She saw him walking into town
from the other side of the bridge.

An adventurer.

The sword, the armor,
he had to be an adventurer.

The adventurer had come because
a monster had been seen in the mountains
and the villagers feared it would not be
long until it made its way down into the town.

The adventurer was
to go into the mountains and slay the beast.

The adventurer was headed into town and
the girl followed, trying to get a better look.

Closer and closer
she crept.

Closer and closer
until one swift turn
and the two bumped
right into one another.

Face to face with a real life adventurer
the girl didn't know what to say so she
blurted out everything that came to mind.

"You're an adventurer aren't you? I've always wanted to meet an adventurer. You
have to tell me all about the things you have seen and the places you've been. What
was the worst? Have you seen any dragons? What are dungeons like? Have you seen
the ocean? What are adventures like? I want to know all about what its like. Have you
ever..."

The only pause
came when she was
forced to take a breath.

The adventurer had been far and wide and had never seen anything quite like the strange green girl.

He had also never met anyone so genuinely interested in all things adventurer.
The pause for breath gave an opening to get a word in edgewise.

"Would you like to go on an adventure with me?"

What could the girl say?
"Yes!"

And so it was decided.

The two would go on an adventure together.

They set out at the crack of dawn the very next day.

The hike into the mountains was rough going
and took hours.

They walked in silence at first neither
knowing quite what to say.
But before long they had struck up a
conversation and the journey seemed easier for it.

As they walked down the road into the woods,
to the path in the hills, to the trail in the mountains
the girl asked many questions about all the
adventurer had seen and done.

The adventurer was more than happy
to share his tale with someone so interested.

They walked and talked
and became fast friends.

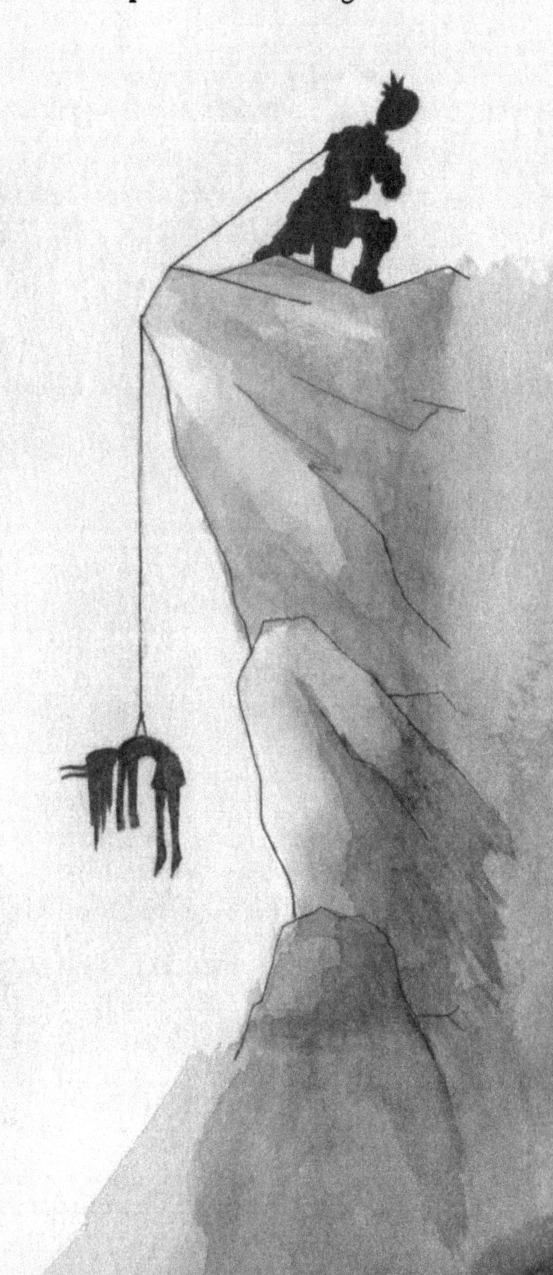

Over boulder
and up cliff they went.

Until at long last they came
to the lair of the beast.

No sooner had they arrived than
the two were set upon by the beast.

It had smelled them coming.

The battle raged for what seemed like forever.

Going this way and that.

All over the top of the mountain.

Until at long last the pair had bested the beast.

They lay on the ground looking up at the sky for a time.

It was important to appreciate the day having so narrowly escaped death. So said the adventurer

The trek back to town was easier now that there was no daunting task ahead of them.

Trail to path, path to road they went
until they made their way back to town.

A crowd of townsfolk had gathered
and swept the adventurer up in a
flurry of celebration.

The girl was left alone.

The next morning the girl did all the things she
normally did feeling
sure that the adventurer
would have left by now,
moving on to bigger
and better things.

But he hadn't left.
Not yet.

He still had a very important question to ask the girl.

"I have been far and wide and I have never met someone like you. Even after all these years, after countless adventures you managed to make it fun again."

"Would you like to go on ever so very many more adventures with me?"

The two set out the very next day
and the girl never looked back.

The End.